GANESHA is just like any other kid, except that he has the head of an elephant and rides around on a magical mouse. And he **loves** sweets, especially the traditional dessert **laddoo.** But when Ganesha insists on biting into a super jumbo jawbreaker **laddoo,** his tusk breaks off! Ganesha is terribly upset, but with the help of the wise poet Vyasa, he learns that what seems broken can actually be quite useful after all.

The bold, bright colors of India leap right off the page in this fresh and funny picture book adaptation of how Ganesha came to write the epic poem of Hindu literature, the **Mahabharata.** With vibrant, graphic illustrations, expressive characters, and off-beat humor, this is a wonderfully inventive twist on a classic tale.

Praise for Ganesha's Sweet Tooth

"Pink elephants haven't looked this good since 'Dumbo.'" —*The New York Times*

"Beautifully presented. . . . So sweet we almost want to pop it in our mouths."
—*Entertainment Weekly*

"Stylish. . . . A fresh and comedic introduction to a Hindu legend, with a winning combination of both eye candy and actual candy." —*Publishers Weekly*

"Bright, elaborately detailed illustrations. . . . Grade-schoolers . . . will enjoy the story's turnarounds and focus on luscious sweets, and many will be ready for the classic Hindu myth."
—*Booklist*

An Ezra Jack Keats New Illustrator Honor Book
A New York Public Library Title for Reading and Sharing
An IRA Notable Books for a Global Society Award winner
A Georgia Children's Book Award nominee

Super jumbo thanks
to Julie Romeis,
Amy Achaibou,
Adobe Illustrator,
and Neutraface.

First Chronicle Books LLC
paperback edition, published
in 2015. Originally published
in hardcover in 2012 by
Chronicle Books LLC.

The
Library
of Congress
has cataloged
the previous edition
under
ISBN 978-1-4521-0362-4.

Typeset
in Neutra Demi.
The illustrations in
this book were rendered
in Adobe Illustrator.

Manufactured in China.

10 9 8 7 6

Chronicle Books LLC
680 Second Street
San Francisco
California
94107

www.chroniclekids.com

To all my nieces and nephews. Be sure to share your laddoos. **—Sanjay**

To my mom and dad, for giving me a love of books, and everything else. **—Emily**

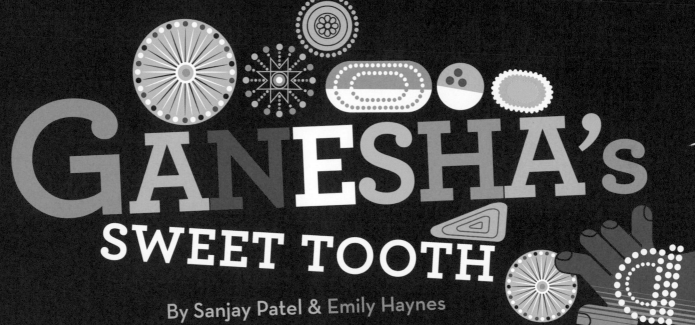

GANESHA's
SWEET TOOTH

By Sanjay Patel & Emily Haynes

Illustrated by Sanjay Patel

chronicle books·san francisco

GANESHA

is a Hindu god.
He's very important
and powerful. And a
tad chubby.

But when he was a kid,
he was just like any
other kid . . .

except that he had an
elephant's head and cruised around
on a magical mouse collecting fruit, rice, sweets,
and other gifts from the temples in his neighborhood.

Ganesha loved to eat sweets and candy, especially the traditional Indian dessert **laddoo.**

His best friend, Mr. Mouse, could eat only one at a time, which
was okay by Ganesha. He didn't want to share **all his laddoos!**
"Squeak!"

One day while Ganesha and Mr. Mouse were out looking for sweets, they discovered a new kind of **laddoo** . . .

THE SUPER JUMBO
JAWBREAKER LADDOO!

Ganesha snatched up the shiny treat
and was about to eat it right
there on the spot.

"Wait!"

squeaked Mr. Mouse.

"Don't eat it! It's a

JAWBREAKER!

It'll break your tusk!"

"But I'm a god," said Ganesha.
"I'm invincible."

Ganesha popped the **laddoo** in his mouth.
He bit down, and . . .

SNAP!

"Squeak! Oh, no!" Mr. Mouse yelled.

"How will I ever put my tusk back on?" Ganesha wailed.

Ganesha was very clever and tried all sorts of ideas. . . .

"What if I tie it on with string? What if I stick it on with glue?
Maybe I could just hold it on with my hand?"

But nothing worked.

"I look lopsided!"
he said. "Everyone will laugh at me."

"No, they won't," said Mr. Mouse. "Everyone loses their teeth. And besides, you already have an elephant's head and your friends still love you."

Ganesha wasn't convinced. He thought he looked awful. He took all his anger and frustration and hurled his tusk at the moon. But the tusk didn't hit the moon.

It sailed over a bush and hit the head of an old man who was walking by!

"Is this your tusk?" the old man asked.

"I'm sorry," said Ganesha. "I didn't mean to hit you. I was aiming for the moon."

"What's your name?"

"I'm Ganesha and this is Mr. Mouse."

"You're Ganesha?!" the old man exclaimed. "I've been looking for you.

I'm Vyasa, the poet, and I need a special scribe for a poem. It's so long that no man could ever write the whole thing—all the pens in the world would break before it was done."

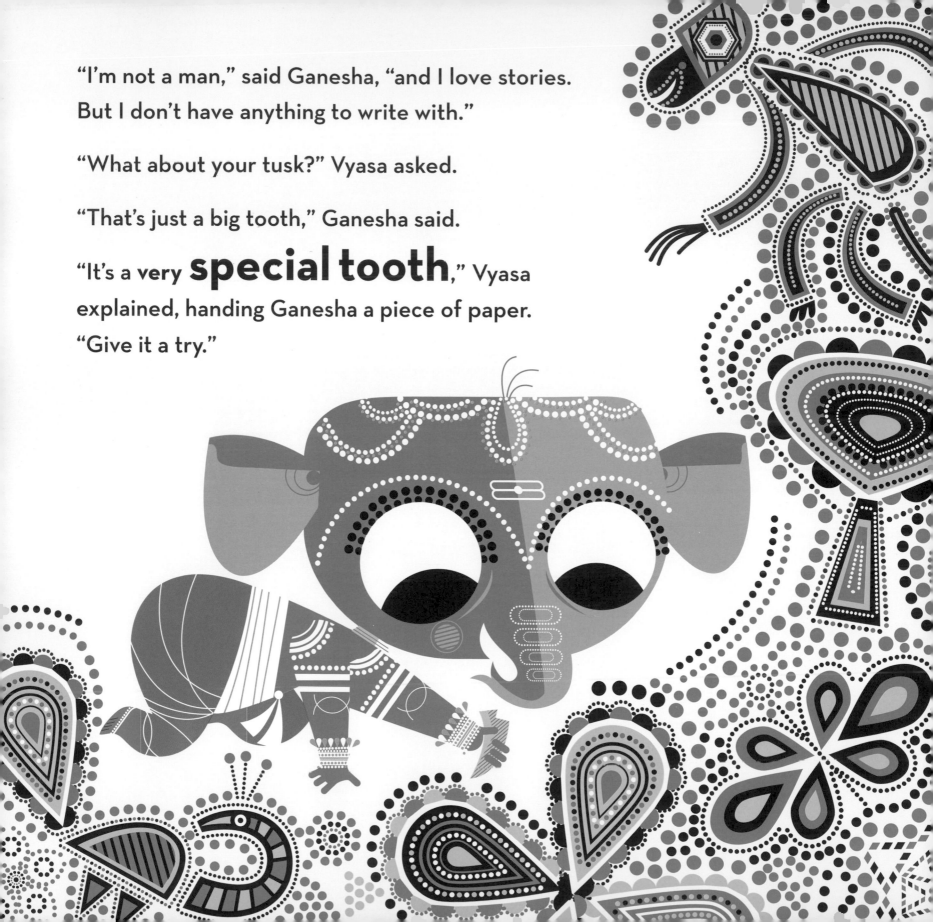

"I'm not a man," said Ganesha, "and I love stories. But I don't have anything to write with."

"What about your tusk?" Vyasa asked.

"That's just a big tooth," Ganesha said.

"It's a very **special tooth**," Vyasa explained, handing Ganesha a piece of paper. "Give it a try."

Ganesha took the paper and pressed down with the tip of his tusk. It made a mark! Ganesha was so excited that he drew a flower, and a tree, and a picture of Mr. Mouse, along with a few of his other favorite things.

"I LOVE my tusk!"

said Ganesha. "I'd be happy to help you. What is the story about?"

"The beginning of things," said Vyasa. "It's rather hard to sum up. It's called the **Mahabharata**."

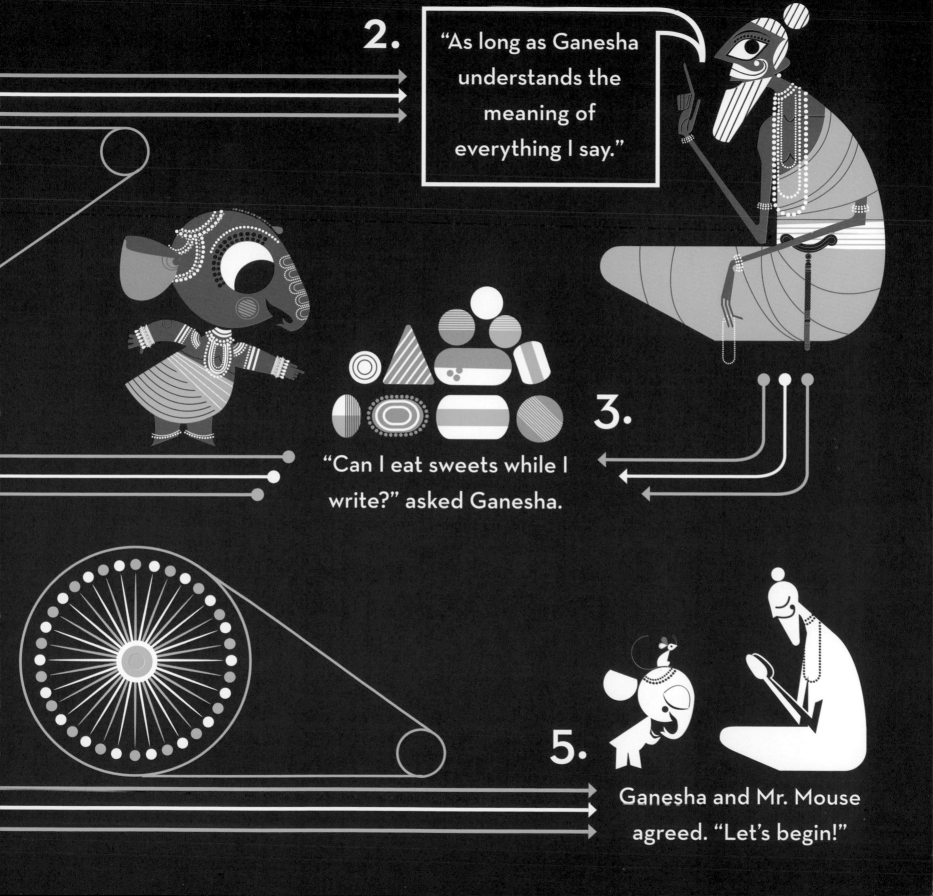

As Vyasa spoke, Ganesha put his tusk to the paper and began writing. Soon he forgot all about the **super jumbo jawbreaker laddoo** and how funny he looked. He even forgot about the sweets he wanted to eat.

"Long ago," Vyasa said, "there lived a very brave king of Hastinapur. One day when he was out hunting, he happened upon a beautiful woman sitting on the banks of the Ganga River . . ."

One hundred thousand verses later, Ganesha put down his tusk. The **Mahabharata**—the great epic of Hindu literature—was complete.

Ganesha peeked around a stack of paper and saw that
Mr. Mouse had been eating his way through the **laddoos**
as they worked—the poem had taken a very long time!

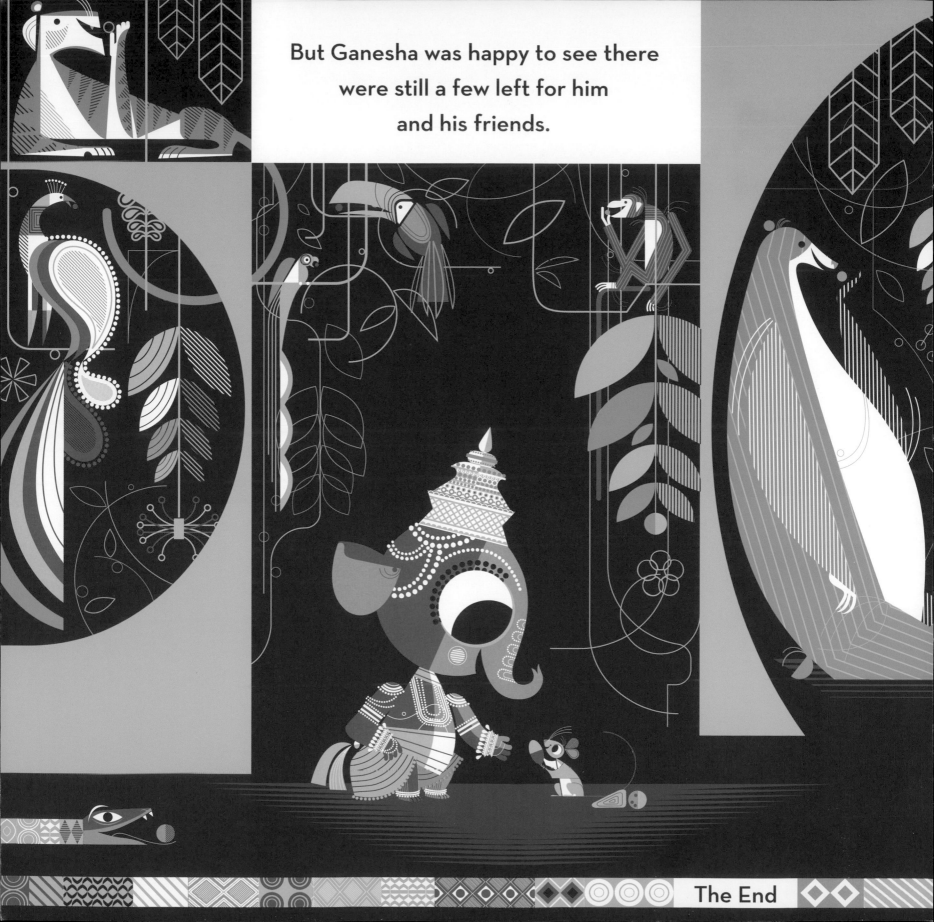

But Ganesha was happy to see there were still a few left for him and his friends.

The End

Authors' Note

The story of how Ganesha broke his tusk is one of the most popular legends in Hindu mythology. In it, the poet Vyasa asks the great god Ganesha to transcribe the **Mahabharata**, which is an ancient epic Sanskrit poem. Ganesha agrees to help as long as Vyasa can recite the poem without stopping. Vyasa agrees with the condition that Ganesha understand everything he says before he writes it down. Soon after they begin, Ganesha's pen breaks. In order to keep writing, clever Ganesha quickly breaks off his tusk and uses that to finish recording the tale. From then on, Ganesha was also known as Ekadanta, the one-toothed god.

Ganesha's Sweet Tooth is not a retelling of this classic legend, though it is loosely based on the story. Some elements and scenes in this book are not found in Hindu mythology (the super jumbo jawbreaker **laddoo**!), and we changed certain plot points to develop an original and, we hope, fun picture book. Our wish is that readers will be entertained and enchanted by Ganesha and Mr. Mouse and that they'll be inspired to learn even more about the rich and varied stories of Hindu mythology.

For young readers (and adults) who are unfamiliar with the few foreign words in the story, here is a guide to the most common pronunciations: **Laddoo**: LA-du; **Mahabharata**: muh-HAH-BAHR-uh-tuh; **Ganesha**: guh-NAY-shuh; **Vyasa**: vee-YA-sha.

—Sanjay Patel & Emily Haynes

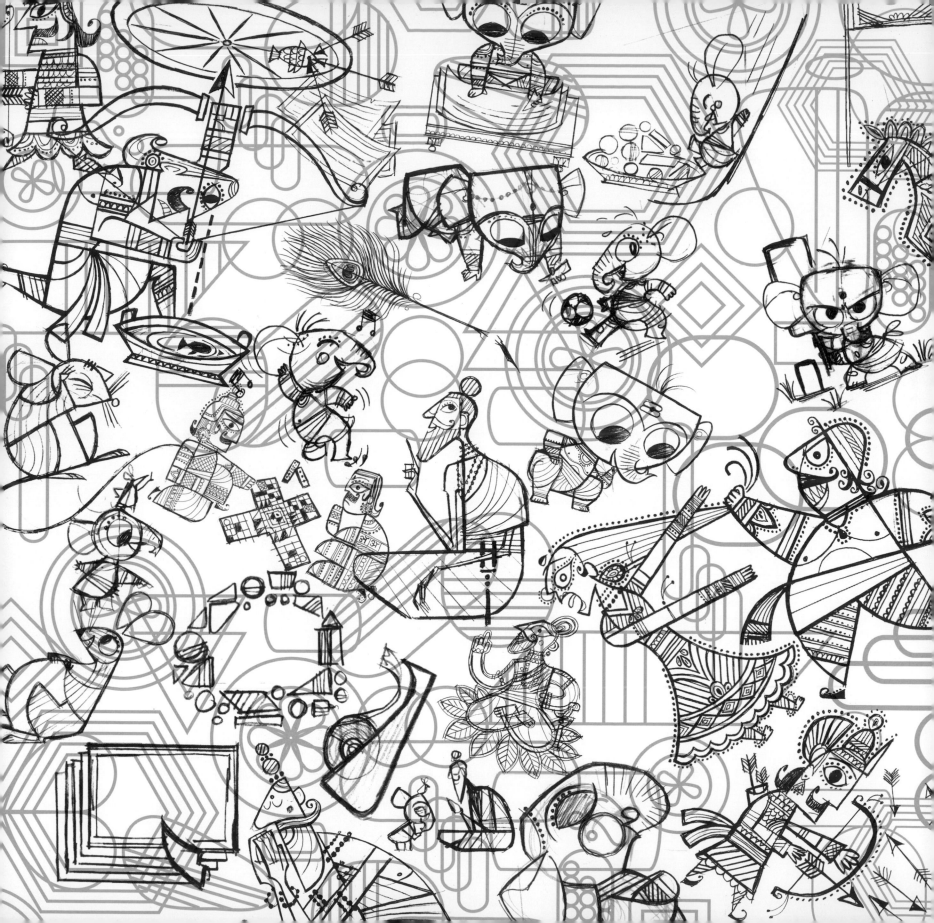

SANJAY PATEL is an animator, storyboard artist, and short film director for Pixar Animation Studios, where he has worked on many features including **A Bug's Life**, **Ratatouille**, **The Incredibles**, and **Cars 2**. Sanjay is also the creator of **Ramayana: Divine Loophole**, **The Big Poster Book of Hindu Deities**, and **The Little Book of Hindu Deities**. He lives in Oakland, California. Learn more about Sanjay at Gheehappy.com.

EMILY HAYNES is an editor by day, specializing in entertainment, animation, and humor titles, and a writer and dreamer by night. In her spare time she can be found reading books to her two-year-old son. This is her first children's book. She lives in Oakland, California.